D1081136

Beetle and the Bear

Beetle and Friends

Get together with Beetle and his friends!

Be sure to read:

Beetle and the Hamster

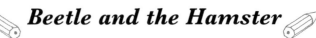

... and lots, lots more!

Beetle and the Bear

Hilary McKay
illustrated by Lesley Harker

SCHOLASTIC

For Matthew Hipkin with love – H.M.

Scholastic Children's Books,
Commonwealth House, 1-19 New Oxford Street,
London, WC1A 1NU, UK
a division of Scholastic Ltd
London ~ New York ~ Toronto ~ Sydney ~ Auckland
Mexico City ~ New Delhi ~ Hong Kong

First published by Scholastic Ltd, 2002

Text copyright © Hilary McKay, 2002
Illustrations copyright © Lesley Harker, 2002

ISBN 0 439 99444 6

Printed and bound by Oriental Press, Dubai, UAE

10 9 8 7 6 5 4 3 2 1

The rights of Hilary McKay and Lesley Harker to be identified as the author
and illustrator of this work respectively have been asserted by them in accordance
with the Copyright, Designs and Patents Act, 1988.

Chapter One

It was the day before the start of the new school year. Next day would be Beetle's first day of school. Beetle and his big brother Max were upstairs in their bedroom.

Max was sorting out his football kit.
Beetle was lying on the floor with his socks
off and his face buried in the stomach of
his old brown bear. He was humming a
terrible home-made song. It had no words
and it had no tune, it was just a noise.
A loud noise.

"I wish you would shut up," said Max.
Beetle hummed louder than ever, deep
and damp in the middle of his bear.

Max leaned over
and dropped his
football boots on
Beetle's head.

Beetle added some moans
to his song. It became
a moaning song.
It sounded awful.

Max poured paint water into a paper bag.
He twisted the top of the bag shut and
placed it gently down
the neck of Beetle's
T-shirt.

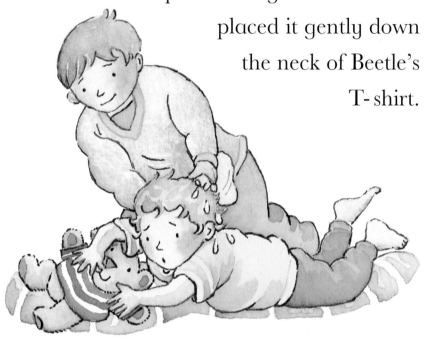

Paint water seeped down Beetle's back,
trickling coldly between
his shoulder blades.
His song became
a wail and then
stopped. He sat
up and cried a bit,
rocking his bear.

"You two!" called their mother from the hall below. "Do I have to come up?"

"No!" yelled back Max and Beetle together.

"Are you fighting?"

"Course not!" shouted Max, and Beetle yelled, "We never fight!"

"Huh!" said their mother, but she did not come up.

Max was seven, going on eight. He was tall and grown up and captain of the Junior Football Team. He had a best friend called Mike who was in the football team too.

Max worried a lot about Beetle. He did not know how Beetle would manage school.

Beetle was five. He
was useless at football.
He sucked his
thumb.

He cried whenever he
wanted to. He liked to
take his socks off and
fiddle with his toes.

Worst of all he had an
old brown bear called
Bear that he carted
around with him
everywhere he went.

At playschool they had put up with Beetle, and his tears and his bear. They said he would grow up One Day.

Max thought school was going to be a very big shock for Beetle.

"It's going to be a lot, lot different from playschool," he told him.

"I know."

"You won't be able to suck your thumb."

"I know."

"Or muck about with your toes."

"I know."

"Or sing your awful songs."

"I know."

"Or take your bear."

"I'm taking my bear," said Beetle.

Chapter Two

Beetle's bear was as old as Beetle. He had
worn out brown fur and a chewed up nose.
He had kind brown eyes and a red and
white football jumper. Beetle squashed
Bear into his new school bag and took it
to show Max.

"Look how well
he fits!" said Beetle.

"Beetle," said Max. "You'll get laughed
at. You'll get really laughed at! Don't take
your bear."

Beetle took no notice. The first day of term
came and Beetle took his bear.

At school Beetle's teacher, Mrs Holiday, told Beetle to share a table with a boy called Henry.

They were the two smallest boys in the class. Henry was very excited about being at school. He was always bouncing up and asking questions. Beetle did not bounce or ask questions. Beetle sulked.

For the first week of school Beetle managed to keep Bear a secret. He kept him in his school bag which was hung up in the cloakroom.

Whenever he got lonely or bored he would put up his hand and ask to go to the toilet. Then he would hurry off to the cloakroom and rub his cheek against Bear's kind brown face. It made him feel much better.

Walking home from school on Friday afternoon Max said to Beetle, "Have you made friends with anyone yet?"

"No," said Beetle crossly. "I don't like any of them and none of them like me!"

"Mike and me made friends on our first day," said Max.

"It's easy for you," said Beetle even more crossly. "Everyone likes you! You always have someone to play with."

"I play football with Mike and the rest of the team, that's all," said Max.

"Could I be on the team?" asked Beetle. "I'm the right age. And you are team captain! You could make the others let me."

"Beetle," said Max patiently. "You know you can never kick the ball!"

"I can," said Beetle, "if it's standing still. And I'm standing still. And nobody shouts."

"Come into the garden and practise," said
Max. "You need a lot of practice."

"I don't want to practise," said Beetle.
"I want to be on the team!
You even let girls!"

"Not if they won't practise and can't kick
the ball unless it's standing still and they're
standing still and nobody is shouting!"

Beetle put his thumb in his mouth and let himself cry a bit.

"I'll try and think of something to help," said Max kindly. "And you'll soon make friends with someone. What about Henry who you sit next to?"

"I only sit there because the teacher made me," said Beetle.

"Oh," said Max.

"And Henry sits there because she made him."

"Oh."

"I call him Horrible Henry. Secretly. In my head. He ate my rubber. My new stripy rubber. He eats rubbers all the time."

"Oh," said Max.

✏️ Chapter Three ✏️

Henry reminded Beetle of a hamster.
A small, tough, rubber-eating, nose-into-
everything hamster. He asked questions all
the time.

"Max is good at football, isn't he?" he said on Monday afternoon. "Why doesn't he teach you? Has he ever asked you if I'd like to be on the team?"

"NO,"
said Beetle.

"Why do you keep going to the toilet so often? Why is your school bag always stuffed so full? What's it got inside? Spare pants?"

"NO,"
said Beetle.

Henry did not give up. He asked why
Beetle was singing awful made-up songs,
and why he had taken his socks
off (Beetle hastily pulled them
back on again) and why
he was sucking
his thumb.

Then Henry was told off by Mrs Holiday
for talking too much
and for making
Beetle cry.
   "I don't
care," said
Henry.
"Beetle's
a big wet
drip!"

Really Henry did care.
He cared a lot. He was
very cross with Beetle for
crying and getting him
into trouble. As soon
as he could he went
off to the cloakroom
on a pretend toilet visit.

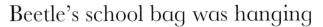

Beetle's school bag was hanging
on Beetle's peg,
bulging and
unguarded.
Henry looked
inside and
discovered
Beetle's
bear.

When he came back he was grinning.
He whispered, "Hey Beetle! Guess what
I saw in the cloak—"

"HENRY!" said Mrs Holiday in such
an awful voice that Henry
shut up for the
rest of the
afternoon.

At the end of school, Mrs Holiday asked Beetle to stay behind a minute and help her water the plants. That was supposed to be a treat but it did not please Beetle. He had an awful feeling that he knew what Henry had seen out in the cloakroom.

Beetle watered the plants so fast he flooded the windowsills and then he rushed out to the cloakroom.

The first thing he saw was
his school bag hanging flat
and empty.

Then he heard screams
of laughter coming from
the playground.

Through the open door Beetle saw
Horrible Henry, swinging Bear round and
round his head.

"Beetle's brought his teddy bear!" sang Horrible Henry, dancing up and down.

Blazing with fury Beetle rushed at Henry.

"Beetle's got a teddy!" sang Henry, and he threw Bear to Kirsty, a noisy little girl with red pigtails.

Before Beetle could get to her, Kirsty had thrown Bear across the playground to somebody else. Then Henry got him again and twirled around in front of Beetle, wearing Bear like a hat.

"Beetle's brought his teddy bear!" sang Henry.

"Throw him to me! To me! To me!" cried at least half a dozen people, and Bear went sailing up into the air again.

It was like a terrible game of pig in the middle, with Bear the ball and Beetle the pig.

And the more Beetle ran and cried and hit and shouted the more everyone laughed.

"BEETLE'S BROUGHT HIS TEDDY BEAR!" they sang. "BEETLE'S GOT A TEDDY!"

All of a sudden Max came charging out of school, with Mike behind him.

Max saw in one glance what had happened.

He saw Beetle with his eyes and nose running, and poor old Bear, more battered than ever, flying across the playground in his grubby red and white football jumper.

All at once Max knew what to do.

He charged into the middle of the children and yelled, "WHAT ARE YOU KIDS DOING WITH OUR TEAM MASCOT?"

Chapter Four

There was a stunned silence in the
playground. Beetle stared at his brother in
amazement. Henry looked as if he had just
been slapped. Max's friend Mike, who knew
all about Beetle's bear, retrieved Bear from
Kirsty and handed him to Beetle.

"Our only team mascot!" said Max loudly to Mike. "And the big match on Saturday and they chuck him about like a teddy!"

"Is he all right, Beet?" asked Mike. Beetle nodded.

"We didn't know he was the team mascot," mumbled Kirsty, her cheeks bright red.

"We thought he was just Beetle's bear," said Horrible Henry.

"Beetle," said Max solemnly, "is the Junior Team Mascot Keeper! Isn't he, Mike?"

"Absolutely," said Mike.

"That bear is the Junior Football Team Mascot! And he's got to be looked after! We haven't got a substitute."

"No," agreed Mike, shaking his head. "No, we haven't."

Horrible Henry, who was never squashed for long, suddenly shot up his hand as if Max was a teacher. "You ought to have a substitute!" he said. "You ought, Max! If you like I could bring my bear!"

"What bear's that then?" asked Max, but Henry's reply was drowned out in the din of the rest of Class 1, eagerly offering their bears as Substitute Mascots.

"Sounds like they've all got teddies," said Mike, grinning at Beetle.

"I don't know if we want a Substitute Mascot," said Max, being awkward.

"Mascots are special. You can't just go out and buy one."

"It's got to be a properly looked after bear," agreed Mike.

"Beetle keeps that bear in his bed every night!" Max told Henry impressively.

"I keep my Whitey in my bed every night!" said Henry. "And I've had him for years. He's a really special bear!"

Then most of Class 1 started shouting about their special bears. Max looked at Mike, and Mike looked at Max and they said they would discuss it with the team.

Chapter Five

That was how the teddy bears came to be at school. Old bears, special bears, slept-with-every-night bears. All bears whose owners hoped to be the Junior Football Team Substitute Mascot Keeper.

Max and Mike and Beetle inspected them all, and Henry's won.

Henry's bear was the best. The most worn out. The most slept-with-looking. Also he had a red and white striped football jumper which Henry's gran had stayed up till midnight to knit.

And Max and Mike and
Beetle and the rest of the
football team said it did not
matter at all that Henry's
mum had once washed
him with a pair of red socks so that Whitey
was now a faint but definite pink.

School got much better for Beetle after
that. He and Henry sat together, droning
and chattering and sucking their thumbs
and eating their rubbers.

They took it in turns
to nip out to the
cloakroom to check
on the Mascot and
the Substitute Mascot.

And when the football
team was photographed they were allowed
to be in the picture. Beetle and Henry sat
side by side, right in the middle, grinning
very proudly and holding their bears.